TEN
TALL TALES
By Dr. Seuss

ZAX ByPass

Collins

An imprint of HarperCollinsPublishers

Ten Tall Tales by Dr. Seuss
™ & © Dr. Seuss Enterprises, L.P. 1999
All rights reserved
This edition published in 2000 for Dealerfield Limited.
First published by Random House Inc, New York, USA
This omnibus edition first published 1999 by
HarperCollins*Children's Books*
A Division of HarperCollins*Publishers* Ltd
77-85 Fulham Palace Road, London W6 8JB

The HarperCollins website address is:
www.**fire**and**water**.com

2 4 6 8 10 9 7 5 3 1

ISBN 000 760628 1

Printed and bound in Singapore

CONTENTS

★

THE SNEETCHES

Now, the Star-Belly Sneetches
Had bellies with stars.
The Plain-Belly Sneetches
Had none upon thars.

Those stars weren't so big. They were really so small
You might think such a thing wouldn't matter at all.

But, because they had stars, all the Star-Belly Sneetches
Would brag, "We're the best kind of Sneetch on the beaches."
With their snoots in the air, they would sniff and they'd snort
"We'll have nothing to do with the Plain-Belly sort!"
And whenever they met some, when they were out walking,
They'd saunter straight past them without even talking.

When the Star-Belly children went out to play ball,
Could a Plain Belly get in the game...? Not at all.
You only could play if your bellies had stars
And the Plain-Belly children had none upon thars.

When the Star-Belly Sneetches had frankfurter roasts
Or picnics or parties or marshmallow toasts,
They never invited the Plain-Belly Sneetches.
They left them out cold, in the dark of the beaches.
They kept them away. Never let them come near.
And that's how they treated them year after year.

Then ONE day, it seems...while the Plain-Belly Sneetches
Were moping and doping alone on the beaches,
Just sitting there wishing their bellies had stars...
A stranger zipped up in the strangest of cars!

"My friends," he announced in a voice clear and keen,
"My name is Sylvester McMonkey McBean.
And I've heard of your troubles. I've heard you're unhappy.
But I can fix that. I'm the Fix-it-Up Chappie.
I've come here to help you. I have what you need.
And my prices are low. And I work at great speed.
And my work is one hundred per cent guaranteed!"

McB.

Sylvester
McMonkey
McBean

Then, quickly, Sylvester McMonkey McBean
Put together a very peculiar machine.
And he said, "You want stars like a Star-Belly Sneetch...?
My friends, you can have them for three dollars each!"

"Just pay me your money and hop right aboard!"
So they clambered inside. Then the big machine roared
And it klonked. And it bonked. And it jerked. And it berked
And it bopped them about. But the thing really worked!
When the Plain-Belly Sneetches popped out, they had stars!
They actually did. They had stars upon thars!

Then they yelled at the ones who had stars at the start,
"We're exactly like you! You can't tell us apart.
We're all just the same, now, you snooty old smarties!
And now we can go to your frankfurter parties."

"Good grief!" groaned the ones who had stars at the first.
"We're *still* the best Sneetches and they are the worst.
But, now, how in the world will we know," they all frowned,
"If which kind is what, or the other way round?"

Then up came McBean with a very sly wink
And he said, "Things are not quite as bad as you think.
So you don't know who's who. That is perfectly true.
But come with me, friends. Do you know what I'll do?
I'll make you, again, the best Sneetches on beaches
And all it will cost you is ten dollars eaches."

"Belly stars are no longer in style," said McBean.

"What you need is a trip through my Star-*Off* Machine.

This wondrous contraption will take *off* your stars

So you won't look like Sneetches who have them on thars."

And that handy machine

Working very precisely

Removed all the stars from their tummies quite nicely.

Then, with snoots in the air, they paraded about
And they opened their beaks and they let out a shout,
"We know who is who! Now there isn't a doubt.
The best kind of Sneetches are Sneetches without!"

Then, of course, those with stars all got frightfully mad.
To be wearing a star now was frightfully bad.
Then, of course, old Sylvester McMonkey McBean
Invited *them* into his Star-Off Machine.

Then, of course from THEN on, as you probably guess,
Things really got into a horrible mess.

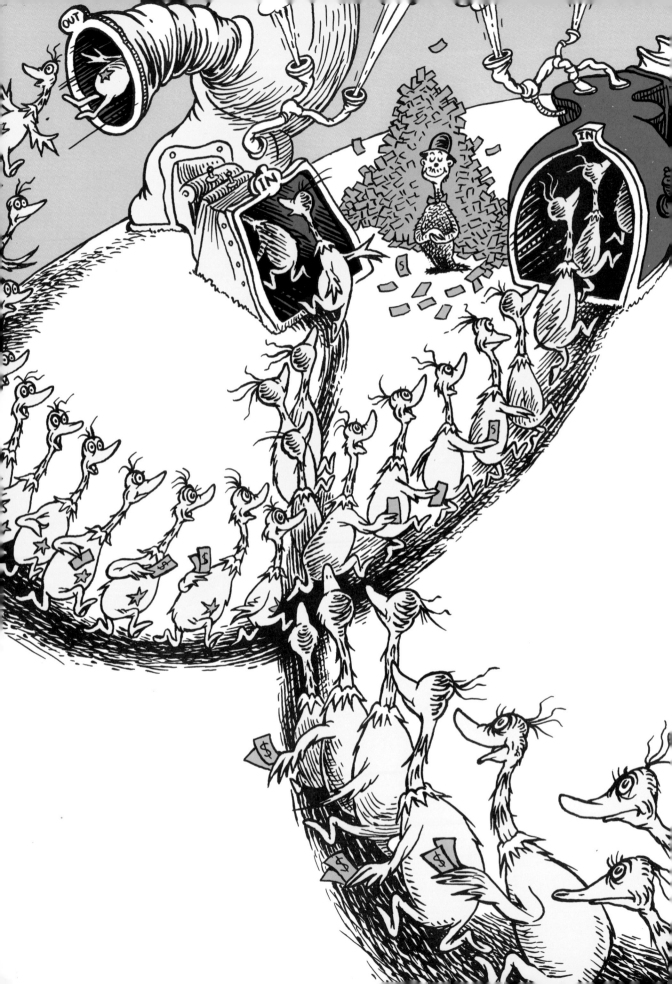

All the rest of that day, on those wild screaming beaches,
The Fix-it-Up Chappie kept fixing up Sneetches.
Off again! On again!
In again! Out again!
Through the machines they raced round and about again,
Changing their stars every minute or two.
They kept paying money. They kept running through
Until neither the Plain nor the Star-Bellies knew
Whether this one was that one ... or that one was this one
Or which one was what one ... or what one was who.

Then, when every last cent
Of their money was spent,
The Fix-it-Up Chappie packed up
And he went.

And he laughed as he drove
In his car up the beach,
"They never will learn.
No. You can't teach a Sneetch!"

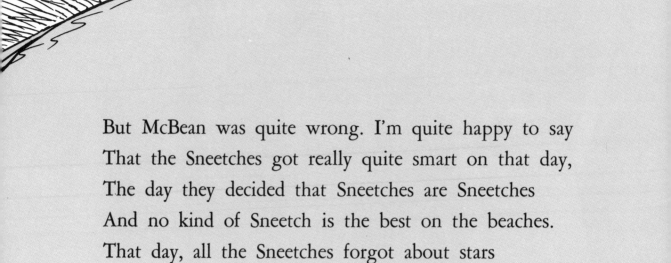

But McBean was quite wrong. I'm quite happy to say
That the Sneetches got really quite smart on that day,
The day they decided that Sneetches are Sneetches
And no kind of Sneetch is the best on the beaches.
That day, all the Sneetches forgot about stars
And whether they had one, or not, upon thars.

For Audrey

I can lick
thirty tigers today!

Well…
Maybe twenty-nine.
You!
Down there!
With the curly hair.
Will you please step out of the line.

I can lick
twenty-nine tigers today….

Well…
That's sort of
A mean thing to do.
I'll cut down my list.
First group is dismissed.
I'll beat up the next twenty-two.

I can lick
Twenty-two tigers today....

Well…
Maybe I'll lick thirteen.
You! In the front row.
You're excused! You may go.
Your fingernails aren't very clean.

I can lick
Thirteen tigers today....

Well . . . .

Quite a few of you seem underweight.
It's not fair, after all,
To lick tigers so small.
I think that I'll only lick eight.

I can lick
Eight big tigers today....

Well…
You look sort of sleepy to me.
Some of you chaps
Should go home and take naps.
I only intend to lick three.

I can lick
Three big tigers today....

Well…
It's frightfully hot
In the sun.
You two, I'm afraid,
Should lie down in the shade.
You're safe.
I shall only lick one.

I can lick
One mighty tiger today....

But…
You know, I have sort of a hunch
That noontime is near.
You just wait for me here.
I'll beat you up right after lunch.

THE
ZAX

One day, making tracks
In the prairie of Prax,
Came a North-Going Zax
And a South-Going Zax.

And it happened that both of them came to a place
Where they bumped. There they stood.
Foot to foot. Face to face.

"Look here, now!" the North-Going Zax said. "I say!
You are blocking my path. You are right in my way.
I'm a North-Going Zax and I always go north.
Get out of my way, now, and let me go forth!"

"Who's in whose way?" snapped the South-Going Zax.
"I always go south, making south-going tracks.
So you're in MY way! And I ask you to move
And let me go south in my south-going groove."

Then the North-Going Zax puffed his chest up with pride.
"I never," he said, "take a step to one side.
And I'll prove to you that I won't change my ways
If I have to keep standing here fifty-nine days!"

"And I'll prove to YOU," yelled the South-Going Zax,
"That I can stand here in the prairie of Prax
For fifty-nine *years!* For I live by a rule
That I learned as a boy back in South-Going School.
Never budge! That's my rule. *Never budge in the least!*
Not an inch to the west! Not an inch to the east!
I'll stay here, not budging! I can and I will
If it makes you and me and the whole world stand still!"

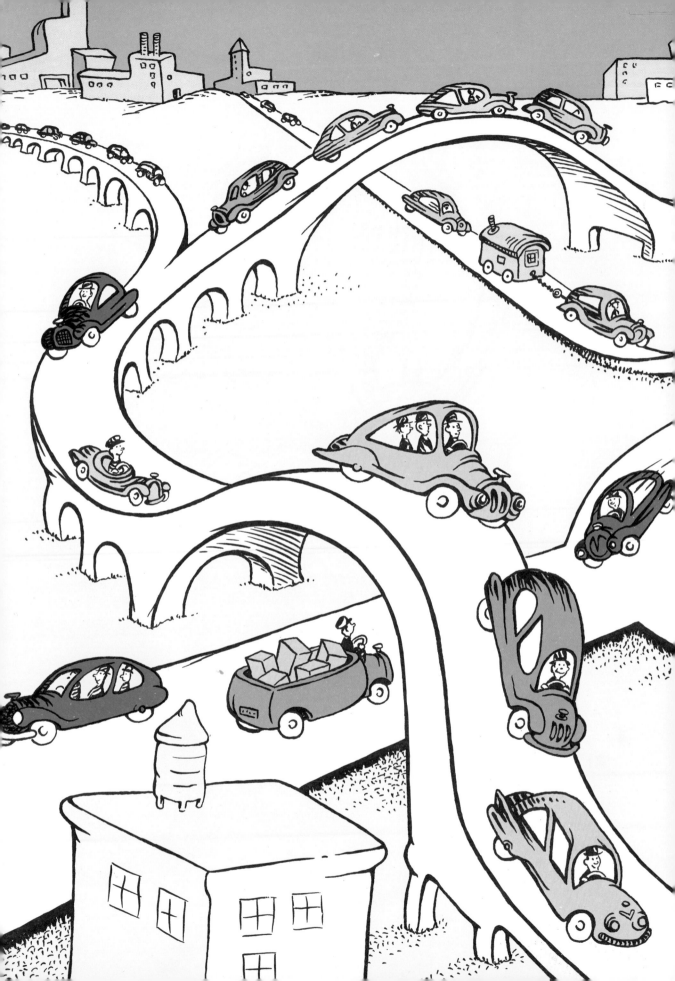

Well ...

Of course the world *didn't* stand still. The world grew.

In a couple of years, the new highway came through

And they built it right over those two stubborn Zax

And left them there, standing un-budged in their tracks.

The rabbit felt mighty important that day
On top of the hill in the sun where he lay.
He felt SO important up there on that hill
That he started to brag, as animals will
And he boasted out loud, as he threw out his chest,
"Of all of the beasts in the world, I'm the best!
On land, and on sea...even up in the sky
No animal lives who is better than I!"

"What's *that*?" growled a voice that was terribly gruff.
"Now why do you say such ridiculous stuff?"
The rabbit looked down and he saw a big bear.
"*I'm* best of the beasts," said the bear. "And so there!"

"You're not!" snapped the rabbit. "I'm better than you!"
"Pooh!" the bear snorted. "Again I say Pooh!
You talk mighty big, Mr. Rabbit. That's true.
But how can you prove it? **Just what can you DO?**"

"Hmmmm..." thought the rabbit,
"Now what CAN I do...?"
He thought and he thought. Then he finally said,
"Mr. Bear, do you see these two ears on my head?
My ears are so keen and so sharp and so fine
No ears in the world can hear further than mine!"

"Humpf!" the bear grunted. He looked at each ear.
"You *say* they are good," said the bear with a sneer,
"But how do *I* know just how far they can hear?"

"I'll prove," said the rabbit, "my ears are the best.
You sit there and watch me. I'll prove it by test."
Then he stiffened his ears till they both stood up high
And pointed straight up at the blue of the sky.
He stretched his ears open as wide as he could.
"*Shhh!* I am listening!" he said as he stood.
He listened so hard that he started to sweat
And the fur on his ears and his forehead got wet.

For seven long minutes he stood. Then he stirred
And he said to the bear, "Do you know what I heard?
Do you see that far mountain . . . ? It's ninety miles off.
There's a fly on that mountain. I just heard him cough!
Now the cough of a fly, sir, is quite hard to hear
When he's ninety miles off. But I heard it quite clear.
So you see," bragged the rabbit, "it's perfectly true
That my ears are the best, so I'm better than you!"

The bear, for a moment, just sulked as he sat
For he knew that *his* ears couldn't hear things like *that*.
"This rabbit," he thought, "made a fool out of me.
Now *I've* got to prove that I'm better than he."
So he said to the rabbit, "You hear pretty well.
You can hear ninety miles. *But how far can you smell?*
I'm the greatest of smellers," he bragged. "See my nose?
This nose on my face is the finest that grows.
My nose can smell *any*thing, both far and near.
With my nose I can smell twice as far as you hear!"

"You can't!" snapped the rabbit.

"I can!" growled the bear

And he stuck his big nose 'way up high in the air.

He wiggled that nose and he sniffed and he snuffed.

He waggled that nose and he whiffed and he whuffed.

For more than ten minutes he snaff and he snuff.

Then he said to the rabbit, "I've smelled far enough."

"All right," said the rabbit. "Come on now and tell
Exactly how far is the smell that you smell?"

"Oh, I'm smelling a *very* far smell," said the bear.
"Away past that fly on that mountain out there.
I'm smelling past many great mountains beyond
Six hundred miles more to the edge of a pond."

"And 'way, 'way out there, by the pond you can't see,
Is a very small farm. On the farm is a tree.
On the tree is a branch. On the branch is a nest,
A very small nest where two tiny eggs rest.
Two hummingbird eggs! Only half an inch long!
But my nose," said the bear, "is so wonderfully strong,
My nose is so good that I smelled without fail
That the egg on the left is a little bit stale!
And *that* is a thing that no rabbit can do.
So you see," the bear boasted, "I'm better than you!
My smeller's so keen that it just can't be beat..."

"What's that?" called a voice
From 'way down by his feet.
The bear and the rabbit looked down at the sound,
And they saw an old worm crawling out of the ground.

"Now, boys," said the worm, "you've been bragging a lot.
You both think you're great. But *I* think you are not.
You're not half as good as a fellow like me.
You hear and you smell. *But how far can you SEE?*
Now, *I'm* here to prove to you big boasting guys
That your nose and your ears aren't as good as my eyes!"

And the little old worm cocked his head to one side
And he opened his eyes and he opened them wide.
And they looked far away with a strange sort of stare
As if they were burning two holes in the air.
The eyes of that worm almost popped from his head.
He stared half an hour till his eyelids got red.
"That's enough!" growled the bear.
"Tell the rabbit and me
How far did you look and just what did you see?"

"Well, boys," the worm answered, "that look that I took
Was a look that looked further than *you'll* ever look!
I looked 'cross the ocean, 'way out to Japan.
For I can see further than anyone can.
There's no one on earth who has eyesight that's finer.
I looked past Japan. Then I looked across China.
I looked across Egypt; then took a quick glance
Across the two countries of Holland and France.
Then I looked across England and, also, Brazil.
But I didn't stop there. I looked much farther still.

"And I kept right on looking and looking until
I'd looked round the world and right back to this hill!
And I saw on this hill, since my eyesight's so keen,
The two biggest fools that have ever been seen!
And the fools that I saw were none other than you,
Who seem to have nothing else better to do
Than sit here and argue who's better than who!"

Then the little old worm gave his head a small jerk
And he dived in his hole and went back to his work.

KING
LOOIE
KATZ

Way back in the olden, golden days
(In the Year One Thirty-Nine)
A fancy cat named Looie
Was the King of Katzen-stein.

King Looie was a proud cat,
Mighty proud of his royal tail.
He had it washed every morning
In a ten-gallon golden pail.

"My tail is such a lovely tail,"
King Looie used to brag.
"My tail must never touch the earth.
My tail must never drag."

So Looie Katz made Fooie Katz
Follow him around.
And Fooie kept the kingly thing
From dragging on the ground.

Well, all was fine in Katzen-stein.
The King's tail wasn't dragging.
But one day Fooie looked behind
And saw that *his* was sagging!

"My lovely tail!" he sighed with pride.
"Oh, this will never do!
If Looie has his tail held up,
I'm going to have mine, too!"

So Fooie Katz made Kooie Katz
Follow him around.
And Kooie Katz kept Fooie's tail
From dragging on the ground.

Now all was fine
In Katzen-stein…
Till Kooie's pride was hurt
When he discovered *his* fine tail
Was dragging in the dirt!

So Kooie made a cat named Chooie
Follow him around,
And Chooie Katz kept Kooie's tail
From dragging on the ground.

And so it went in Katzen-stein.
Next Chooie Katz got Hooie.
And Hooie Katz got Blooie Katz.
And Blooie Katz got Prooie...

...Till all the cats in Katzen-stein
Were hiking round and round,
All keeping one another's tails
From dragging on the ground.

All proud!
Except for one small cat...

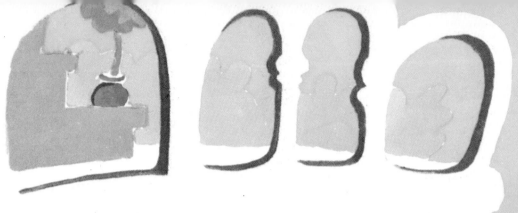

...The last cat in the line.

The last, last cat of all the cats
That lived in Katzen-stein.
A most unhappy little cat
Named Zooie Katzen-bein.

His tail would never be held up.
And poor old Zooie knew it.
Because holding up a cat's tail
Takes another cat to do it.

Poor Zooie got so awfully mad
So mad he could have spit.
But he did a far, far braver thing…

He simply yelled,
"I QUIT!"

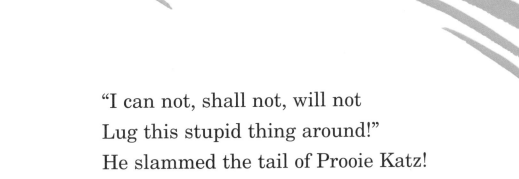

"I can not, shall not, will not
Lug this stupid thing around!"
He slammed the tail of Prooie Katz!
He slammed it on the ground.

Then Prooie Katz slammed Blooie's tail
And Blooie Katz slammed Hooie's.
And Hooie Katz slammed Chooie's tail
And Chooie Katz slammed Kooie's.
All tails in Katzen-stein were slammed
Including proud King Looie's.

And since that day in Katzen-stein,
All cats have been more grown-up.
They're all more demo-catic
Because each cat holds his own up.

WHAT WAS I SCARED OF?

Well...
     I was walking in the night
     And I saw nothing scary.
     For I have never been afraid
     Of anything. Not very.

Then I was deep within the woods
When, suddenly, I spied them.
I saw a pair of pale green pants
With nobody inside them!

I wasn't scared. But, yet, I stopped.
What *could* those pants be there for?
What *could* a pair of pants at night
Be standing in the air for?

And then they moved! Those empty pants!
They kind of started jumping.
And then my heart, I must admit,
It kind of started thumping.

So I got out. I got out fast
As fast as I could go, sir.
I wasn't scared. But pants like that
I did not care for. No, sir.

After that, a week went by.
Then one dark night in Grin-itch
(I had to do an errand there
And fetch some Grin-itch spinach)...
Well, I had fetched the spinach.
I was starting back through town
When those pants raced round a corner
And they almost knocked me down!

I lost my Grin-itch spinach
But I didn't even care.
I ran for home! Believe me,
I had really had a scare!

Now, bicycles were never made
For pale green pants to ride 'em,
Especially spooky pale green pants
With nobody inside 'em!

And the NEXT night, I was fishing
For Doubt-trout on Roover River
When those pants came rowing toward me!
Well, I began to shiver.

And by now I was SO frightened
That, I'll tell you, but I hate to...
I screamed and rowed away and lost
My hook and line and bait, too!

I ran and found a Brickel bush.
I hid myself away.
I got brickels in my britches
But I stayed there anyway.

I stayed all night. The next night, too.
I'd be there still, no doubt,
But I had to do an errand
So, the *next* night, I went out.

I had to do an errand,
Had to pick a peck of Snide
In a dark and gloomy Snide-field
That was almost nine miles wide.

I said, "I do not fear those pants
With nobody inside them."
I said, and said, and said those words.
I said them. But I lied them.

Then I reached inside a Snide bush
And the next thing that I knew,
I felt my hand touch someone!
And I'll bet that you know who.

And there I was! Caught in the Snide!
And in that dreadful place
Those spooky, empty pants and I
Were standing face to face!

I yelled for help. I screamed. I shrieked.
I howled. I yowled. I cried,
"Oh, save me from these pale green pants
With nobody inside!"

But then a strange thing happened.
Why, those pants began to cry!
Those pants began to tremble.
They were just as scared as I!

I never heard such whimpering
And I began to see
That I was just as strange to them
As they were strange to me!

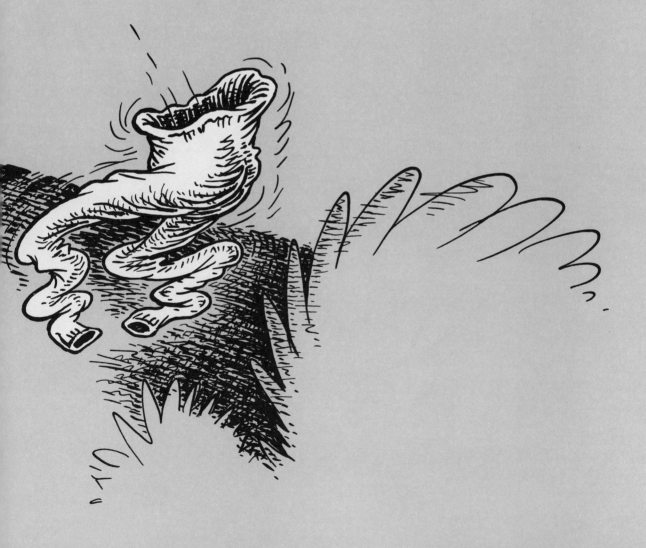

I put my arm around their waist
And sat right down beside them.
I calmed them down.
Poor empty pants
With nobody inside them.

And, now, we meet quite often,
Those empty pants and I,
And we never shake or tremble.
We both smile
And we say
"Hi!"

GERTRUDE McFUZZ

There once was a girl-bird named Gertrude McFuzz
And she had the smallest plain tail ever was.
One droopy-droop feather. That's all that she had.
And, oh! That one feather made Gertrude so sad.
For there was another young bird that she knew,
A fancy young birdie named Lolla-Lee-Lou,
And instead of *one* feather behind, she had *two*!
Poor Gertrude! Whenever she happened to spy
Miss Lolla-Lee-Lou flying by in the sky,
She got very jealous. She frowned. And she pouted.
Then, one day she got awfully cross and she shouted:
"This just isn't fair! I have *one*! She has *two*!
I MUST have a tail just like Lolla-Lee-Lou!"

So she flew to her uncle, a doctor named Dake
Whose office was high in a tree by the lake
And she cried, "Uncle Doctor! Oh, please do you know
Of some kind of a pill that will make my tail grow?"
"Tut tut!" said the doctor. "Such talk! How absurd!
Your tail is just right for your kind of a bird."

Then Gertrude had tantrums. She raised such a din
That finally her uncle, the doctor, gave in
And he told her just where she could find such a pill
On a pill-berry vine on the top of the hill.
"Oh, thank you!" chirped Gertrude McFuzz, and she flew
Right straight to the hill where the pill-berry grew.

Yes! There was the vine! And as soon as she saw it
She plucked off a berry. She started to gnaw it.
It tasted just awful. Almost made her sick.
But she wanted that tail, so she swallowed it quick.
Then she felt something happen! She felt a small twitch
As if she'd been tapped, down behind, by a switch.
And Gertrude looked 'round. And she cheered! It was true!
Two feathers! Exactly like Lolla-Lee-Lou!

Then she had an idea! "Now I know what I'll do . . .
I'll grow a tail *better* than Lolla-Lee-Lou!"

"These pills that grow feathers are working just fine!"
So she nibbled *another* one off of the vine!

She felt a *new* twitch. And then Gertrude yelled, "WHEE!
Miss Lolla has only just *two*! I have *three*!
When Lolla-Lee-Lou sees this beautiful stuff,
She'll fall right down flat on her face, sure enough!
I'll show HER who's pretty! I certainly will!
Why, I'll make my tail even prettier still!"

She snatched at those berries that grew on that vine.
She gobbled down four, five, six, seven, eight, nine!
And she didn't stop eating, young Gertrude McFuzz,
Till she'd eaten three dozen! That's all that there was.

Then the feathers popped out! With a *zang*! With a *zing*!
They blossomed like flowers that bloom in the spring.
All fit for a queen! What a sight to behold!
They sparkled like diamonds and gumdrops and gold!
Like silk! Like spaghetti! Like satin! Like lace!
They burst out like rockets all over the place!
They waved in the air and they swished in the breeze!
And some were as long as the branches of trees.
And *still* they kept growing! They popped and they popped
Until, round about sundown when, finally, they stopped.

"And NOW," giggled Gertrude, "The next thing to do
Is to fly right straight home and show Lolla-Lee-Lou!
And when Lolla sees *these*, why her face will get red
And she'll let out a scream and she'll fall right down dead!"

Then she spread out her wings to take off from the ground,
But, with all of those feathers, she weighed ninety pound!
She yanked and she pulled and she let out a squawk,
But that bird couldn't fly! Couldn't run! Couldn't walk!

And all through that night, she was stuck on that hill,
And Gertrude McFuzz might be stuck up there still
If her good Uncle Dake hadn't heard the girl yelp.
He rushed to her rescue and brought along help.

To lift Gertrude up almost broke all their beaks
And to fly her back home, it took almost two weeks.
And *then* it took almost another week more
To pull out those feathers. My! Gertrude was sore!

And, finally, when all of the pulling was done,
Gertrude, behind her, again had just one...
That one little feather she had as a starter.
But now that's enough, because now she is smarter.

THE GLUNK THAT GOT THUNK

A thing my sister likes to do
Some evenings after supper,
Is sit upstairs in her small room
And use her Thinker-Upper.

She turns her Thinker-Upper on.
She lets it softly purr.
It thinks up friendly little things
With smiles and fuzzy fur.

She sometimes does this by the hour.
Then when she's tired of play,
She turns on her UN-Thinker
And un-thinks the things away.

Well . . . . . .

One evening she was thinking up
Some fuzzy little stuff,
And Sister sighed, "This stuff's all right,
But it's not *fun* enough.

"I've got to think up bigger things.
I'll bet I can, you know.
I'll speed my Thinker-Upper up
As fast as it will go!"

"Think! Think!" she cried.
Her Thinker-Upper gave a snorty snore.
It started thunk-thunk-thunking
As it never had before.
With all her might, her eyes shut tight,
She cried, "Thunk-thunk some more!"

Then, BLUNK! Her Thinker-Upper thunked
A double klunker-klunk.
My sister's eyes flew open
And she saw she'd thunked a Glunk!

He was greenish.
Not too cleanish.
And he sort of had bad breath.
"Good gracious!" gasped my sister.
"I have thunked up quite a meth!"

She turned on her UN-Thinker,
Tried to think the Glunk away.
But she found that her UN-Thinker
Didn't seem to work that day.

The Glunk just smiled and said, "Dear child,
You can't Un-thunk a Glunk.
Ask *anyone*. They'll tell you
That a Glunk can't be UN-thunk.

"I'm here to stay forever
In your lovely, lovely home.
And now, with your permission, dear,
I'll use your tele-foam.

"I call my mother every night.
It gives her such great joy.
She lives nine thousand miles away
And I'm her only boy."

"Long distance is expensive!"
Sister cried. "Get off that line!"
But the Glunk dialed Texa-Kota-Cutt
1-2-3-4-0-9.

"Hello, dear mother," gabbed the Glunk.
"I hope you're feeling fine.
And don't worry 'bout the phone bill.
It's all paid by a friend of mine.
I've just called you up to tell you
How I love you. Oh, *I do!*
And today I did some cooking
And I cooked some Glunker Stew.
Let me tell you how I did it.
You may want to make some, too.

"You take a cup of applesauce.
You add a pinch of straw.
You drop in fourteen oysters,
Seven cooked and seven raw.
You beat it to a frazzle
With a special frazzle-spade.
Then you pour it in a rubber boot
Half filled with lemonade.
Then you toss it in the mixer,
Where you spuggle it and spin it...

"Stop!" my sister yelled.
"This costs ten dollars every minute!"

"Money?…Pooh!" The Glunk just laughed.
"Don't think of things like that."
Then he said, "Now, darling mother,
Let me see. Where was I at?
Oh. You take it off the mixer
When the stew is nicely pink.
Then you add a hunk of something…
Hunk of chuck-a-luck, I think.
Then you chuck in chunks of chicklets.
Then you plunk in seven cherries.
And THEN you plunk in, Mother dear,
Three dozen kinds of berries.

"Now, Mother mine, please do this right.
Those berries that you're plunking…
Unless you plunk them with great care…
Will keep the stew from glunking."

"Stop! Stop!" my little sister screamed.
"It's not a funny joke.
My father can't afford this call.
My father will go broke!"

"Now, you keep still!"
The Glunk snapped back.
He kicked her in the shin.
"Don't you interrupt my mother
When she's plunking berries in.

"Now, mother, plunk one berry. Blue.
Now, plunk one berry. Razz.
What's that?…You have no raspberries?…
Oh, everybody has.
But, if you don't have berries, razz,
A Schnutz-berry will do.
You have a Schnutz. I know you have.
Now plunk it in the stew…."

And he went on talking berries
With his dear old darling mother.
He jabbered and he blabbered
One whole hour. And then another!
He talked three hundred dollars' worth.
My sister shook with fright.
"This Glunk might cost us millions!
He might jabber on all night!
My father will be ruined!
We'll be penniless! We're sunk
Unless I can Un-thunk him.
Oh, I MUST Un-thunk this Glunk!"

And that is how I found them.
She was standing there UN-thunking
...The Glunk still talking Glunker Stew...
That Glunk was not Un-glunking!

Could she Un-thunk the Glunk alone?…
It's very doubtful whether.
So I turned on MY Un-thinker.
We Un-thunk the Glunk together.

Then I gave her
Quite a talking to
About her Thinker-Upper.

NOW...
She only
Thinks up fuzzy things
In the evening, after supper.

TOO MANY DAVES

Did I ever tell you that Mrs. McCave
Had twenty-three sons and she named them all Dave?

Well, she did. And that wasn't a smart thing to do.
You see, when she wants one and calls out, "Yoo-Hoo!
Come into the house, Dave!" she doesn't get *one*.
All twenty-three Daves of hers come on the run!

This makes things quite difficult at the McCaves'
As you can imagine, with so many Daves.
And often she wishes that, when they were born,
She had named one of them Bodkin Van Horn
And one of them Hoos-Foos. And one of them Snimm.
And one of them Hot-Shot. And one Sunny Jim.
And one of them Shadrack. And one of them Blinkey.
And one of them Stuffy. And one of them Stinkey.
Another one Putt-Putt. Another one Moon Face.
Another one Marvin O'Gravel Balloon Face.
And one of them Ziggy. And one Soggy Muff.
One Buffalo Bill. And one Biffalo Buff.
And one of them Sneepy. And one Weepy Weed.
And one Paris Garters. And one Harris Tweed.
And one of them Sir Michael Carmichael Zutt
And one of them Oliver Boliver Butt
And one of them Zanzibar Buck-Buck McFate...
But she didn't do it. And now it's too late.

YERTLE THE TURTLE

On the far-away Island of Sala-ma-Sond,
Yertle the Turtle was king of the pond.
A nice little pond. It was clean. It was neat.
The water was warm. There was plenty to eat
The turtles had everything turtles might need.
And they were all happy. Quite happy indeed.

They *were* . . . until Yertle, the king of them all,
Decided the kingdom he ruled was too small.
"I'm ruler," said Yertle, "of all that I see.
But I don't see *enough*. That's the trouble with me.
With this stone for a throne, I look down on my pond
But I cannot look down on the places beyond.
This throne that I sit on is too, too low down.
It ought to be *higher*!" he said with a frown.
"If I could sit high, how much greater I'd be!
What a king! I'd be ruler of all I could see!"

So Yertle, the Turtle King, lifted his hand
And Yertle, the Turtle King, gave a command.
He ordered nine turtles to swim to his stone
And, using these turtles, he built a *new* throne.
He made each turtle stand on another one's back
And he piled them all up in a nine-turtle stack.
And then Yertle climbed up. He sat down on the pile.
What a wonderful view! He could see 'most a mile!

"All mine!" Yertle cried. "Oh, the things I now rule!
I'm king of a cow! And I'm king of a mule!
I'm king of a house! And, what's more, beyond that,
I'm king of a blueberry bush and a cat!
I'm Yertle the Turtle! Oh, marvellous me!
For I am the ruler of all that I see!"

And all through that morning, he sat there up high
Saying over and over, "A great king am I!"
Until round about noon. Then he heard a faint sigh.
"What's *that*?" snapped the king
And he looked down the stack.
And he saw, at the bottom, a turtle named Mack.
Just a part of his throne. And this plain little turtle
Looked up and he said, "Beg your pardon, King Yertle.
"I've pains in my back and my shoulders and knees.
How long must we stand here, Your Majesty, please?"

"SILENCE!" the King of the Turtles barked back.
"I'm king, and you're only a turtle named Mack."

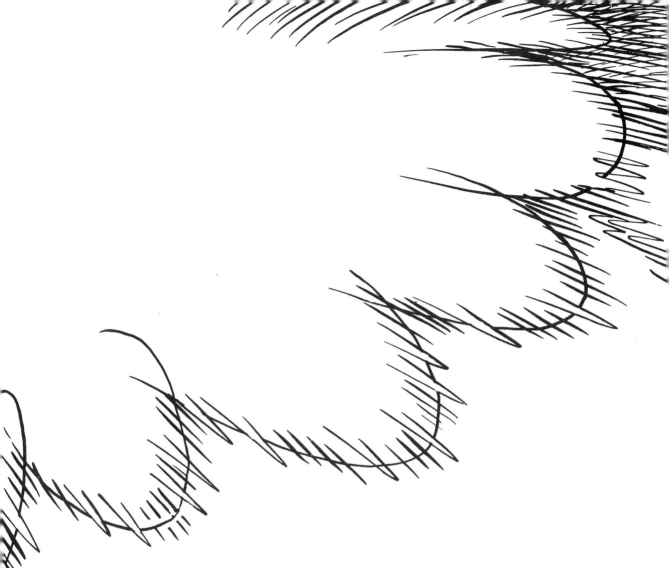

"You stay in your place while I sit here and rule.
I'm king of a cow! And I'm king of a mule!
I'm king of a house! And a bush! And a cat!
But that isn't all. I'll do better than *that*!
My throne shall be *higher*!" his royal voice thundered,
"So pile up more turtles! I want 'bout two hundred!"

"Turtles! More turtles!" he bellowed and brayed.
And the turtles 'way down in the pond were afraid.
They trembled. They shook. But they came. They obeyed.
From all over the pond, they came swimming by dozens.
Whole families of turtles, with uncles and cousins.
And all of them stepped on the head of poor Mack.
One after another, they climbed up the stack.

THEN Yertle the Turtle was perched up so high,
He could see forty miles from his throne in the sky!
"Hooray!" shouted Yertle. "I'm king of the trees!
I'm king of the birds! And I'm king of the bees!
I'm king of the butterflies! King of the air!
Ah, me! What a throne! What a wonderful chair!
I'm Yertle the Turtle! Oh, marvellous me!
For I am the ruler of all that I see!"

Then again, from below, in the great heavy stack,
Came a groan from that plain little turtle named Mack.
"Your Majesty, please...I don't like to complain,
But down here below, we are feeling great pain.
I know, up on top you are seeing great sights,
But down at the bottom we, too, should have rights.
We turtles can't stand it. Our shells will all crack!
Besides, we need food. We are starving!" groaned Mack.

"You hush up your mouth!" howled the mighty King Yertle.
"You've no right to talk to the world's highest turtle.
I rule from the clouds! Over land! Over sea!
There's nothing, no, NOTHING, that's higher than me!"

But, while he was shouting, he saw with surprise
That the moon of the evening was starting to rise
Up over his head in the darkening skies.
"What's THAT?" snorted Yertle. "What IS that thing
That dares to be higher than Yertle the King?
I shall not allow it! I'll go higher still!
I'll build my throne higher! I can and I will!
I'll call some more turtles. I'll stack 'em to heaven!
I need 'bout five thousand, six hundred and seven!"

But, as Yertle, the Turtle King, lifted his hand
And started to order and give the command,
That plain little turtle below in the stack,
That plain little turtle whose name was just Mack,
Decided he'd taken enough. And he had.
And that plain little lad got a little bit mad
And that plain little Mack did a plain little thing.
He burped!
And his burp shook the throne of the king!

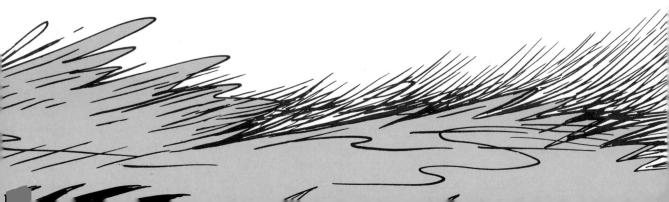

And Yertle the Turtle, the king of the trees,
The king of the air and the birds and the bees,
The king of a house and a cow and a mule...
Well, *that* was the end of the Turtle King's rule!
For Yertle, the King of all Sala-ma-Sond,
Fell off his high throne and fell *Plunk*! in the pond!

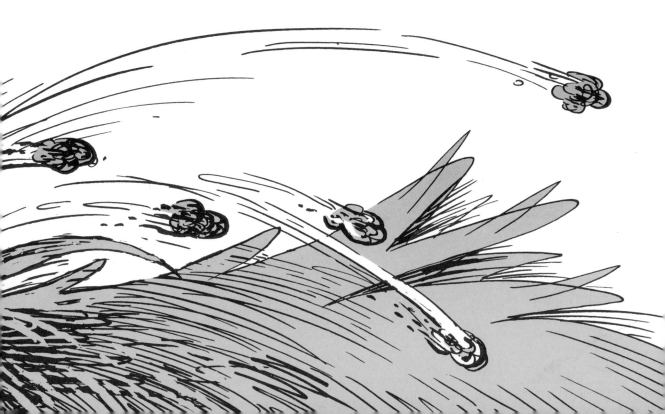

And today the great Yertle, that Marvellous he,
Is King of the Mud. That is all he can see.
And the turtles, of course... all the turtles are free
As turtles and, maybe, all creatures should be.